FALLING GRACE

IT FALLS WHEN YOU LOVE, IT FALLS WHEN YOU FORCE

notionpress.com

FALLING GRACE

IT FALLS WHEN YOU LOVE,
IT FALLS WHEN YOU FORCE

KUNWAR NITIN

notionpress.com

Notion Press

Old No. 38, New No. 6
McNichols Road, Chetpet
Chennai - 600 031

First Published by Notion Press 2016

ISBN 978-93-86073-22-8

Dedicated to all the women on this planet.

and

My newly born baby Saheb.

Contents

ACKNOWLEDGEMENTS

I acknowledge my strength, my inspiration, my guide, my soul – my mother and my father. Smt Asha Kumar and Shri Mukesh Kumar. I grew up in a safe and bright shelter of their love and care. I can never fill their place with any one. My thanks will be like a drop in the ocean. So I have placed my heart and my life at their feet.

I have two immensely beautiful sisters Kamana and Aradhana; thanks to them for loving, caring and helping me throughout as we grew up together.

My younger brother Sachin and his sweet wife Shivani; thanks to them for believing in me and standing by me whenever I needed them.

Thanks to my brothers in-law, Mr O P Rai and Mr Arun Chaudhary for their untold love and blessings.

Special thanks to my nephew Kiyaan. We love each other unconditionally.

Loving thanks to my sister's son Yash, Aadi and naughty Atharva; They are my lovely best buddies. They always make me smile.

My soulful thanks to my Grandmother and my Grandfather, late Smt Sunder Baso Devi and late Shri Harihar Kunwar. My grandmother nurtured me through the first four years of my life and imbibed in me the strength of love, emotions and intense stubbornness towards my goals.

My thanks to my beloved wife Chhaya, She is the main reason behind writing this novel, I knew it eighteen years ago that my passion was writing when I was in twelfth grade, but I decided that I will write only after my marriage.

My sincere thanks to my maternal younger brothers Jeet, Mani, Rumu, Binu, Somu and Sagar; who always stood by my side and elder brothers Rajat, Rishi, Somendra, Saurabh and Ritu; who always showered their love on me.

My thanks to my maternal sisters Munni, Lally, Lilly, Mittu, Mala, Poonam, Milly, Bhanu, crazy Priya, elegant Shreya, cute Honey and calmly beautiful Golu, Mogli and Kirti.

My loving thanks to all my maternal uncles and aunts.

My regards and thanks to my paternal elder brothers, Hemant, Girish, Sirish, Alok, Basant, Vivek and Avinash; with whom I learned and grew old.

My soulful thanks to all my paternal uncles and aunts.

My heartiest thanks to, Vibha, Neelam, Geeta, Kavita, Sarita, Asha, Pammi, Chunni, Shweta, Neetu and Manisha.

Thanks to my sisters in law, Aneeta, Vibha, Poonam, Alpana, Kalpana, Rashmi, Mamta, Savi and Rishika.

My very special thanks to my dear nieces and nephews Rahul, Priyanka, Deepika, Rinki, Pinki, Twinkle, Rolly, Saalin, Yuvraaj, Ishita, Ujjali, Olive and Angel, Mithi; they are gifts of God and my sweet little friends.

Thanks to all my previous girlfriends. I learned so many things from these lovely Ladies.

My thanks to Pushpam and Chintu.

My alcoholic thanks to all my alcoholic friends.

There are many people who loved me and inspired me somehow, somewhere;

Thanks to them.

My heartiest thanks to the entire team at Notion Press, for believing in me.

Thanks to water, air, fire, sky and earth

Thanks to the Almighty, for all that you have provided for me.

Who have remained not thanked, will always remain in my heart.

Love you all.

Chapter - 1
CHARMED

The flight from Lucknow to Kolkata had just landed. It was 4.30 p.m. and the passengers were rushing to check out. I was waiting near the conveyor belt for my bags. I spotted my trolley bag, which was bobbing towards me. I thought life was similar to the conveyor belt. And like the bags, we moved up and down the conveyor belt of life. Thinking so, I walked towards the exit. At a corner, near the exit, was an open lounge bar. I stopped there to refresh myself.

"Hello sir, how was your flight?" the girl behind the counter asked me very politely.

"Hi, it was good," I replied softly.

"Do you want anything?"

"Yes, one large Black Dog."

"On the rocks, water or soda, sir?"

"On the rocks, but fill it with water too."

She smiled and said, "Okay sir. Just a minute."

"No problem."

I looked around. It was a very clean and pleasant environment. People were bustling around.

"Your drink, sir. It's 350."

I gave her 500 rupees and said, "Keep the change."

She smiled in delight.

"Thank you, sir."

"My pleasure."

As I sat on a chair enjoying my drink and the happy surroundings, my mobile phone rang. I answered the call.

"Hello sir, come outside. I am waiting," said the voice on the other end.

"Okay, okay Pandey. I am coming," I replied. I quickly finished my drink and rushed to the exit.

Pandey was a simple man, about forty-five years old. He owned a small private taxi service.

I came outside and saw Pandey waving his hand.

"How are you, sir?"

"Fine, and you Pandey *ji*?"

"Thanks to your blessing, life is running somehow," he replied and grabbed my luggage with affection.

"What happened Pandey *ji*? You look lost."

"Life itself is a problem, sir. My wife is seriously ill. Her kidney is not working. All my money is spent on her dialysis and medicines. Then there are my kids, their studies, food and everything. I am totally frustrated managing my business and their needs," Pandey said agitatedly.

"Oh my God! You are in trouble. But don't worry, everything will be all right. It is all part of life," I said, walking behind him to the car parking.

"Hope so, sir," he replied.

We walked up to Pandey's car—a black Santro.

Pandey placed my luggage in the trunk and we both sat in the front.

"Ashoka hotel, sir?" asked Pandey.

"No, Park Street. I have booked a room in Hotel VIP International," I said.

"But you always stay in Ashoka, sir. Everybody knows you there."

"Yes, but sometimes change is good."

The car ran smoothly. Pandey was a good driver. My eyes were scouring the view outside. Some things were common to every Indian city: beggars, crowds, traffic jams and pollution and Kolkata was no exception. But I loved Kolkata for its tradition, culture, fish, festivals and people. Overall, it was an entertaining city.

Cool soothing breeze, mixed with the lavender aroma of the car perfume, blew through the vents of the air-conditioner. A melodious Ghulam Ali song from the car radio, combined with the after-effect of the premium Scotch whisky I had at the airport, created a heady velvety mood. And I soon drifted into a nap.

We reached the hotel at 6.10 p.m.

After the formalities, I checked into my room. It was a luxurious double-bed room with a mini-bar. I tipped the bellboy generously.

As I plonked into the sofa, Pandey asked me, "May I go now, sir?"

"Oh yes yes, Pandey," I said and paid him ten thousand rupees more than his taxi fare.

Pandey was delighted as he got what he had hoped for.

"This is why everybody loves you, sir," he said, with wet eyes.

"It's all right, Pandey. Don't be emotional. Listen, people gasp for breath while earning money. I spend my money to earn more breathing. It is simple. You know, once I was an asthma patient. So I know the value of breathing. Anything you need, just call me."

"Thank you very much, sir," he said and turned to leave.

"Close the door, Pandey *ji*," I yelled.

I heard the door close.

I fixed a drink and dialed a number.

"Hello. Ghosh Babu, how are you?" I said.

"Oh, hello sir. Fine and you?" Ghosh replied.

"Same. Guess what? I am in Kolkata and I am staying in VIP International," I said.

"Oh my God! What's the room number, sir? I am coming," he said enthusiastically.

I told him my room number and disconnected the call. Ghosh was the managing member of an orchestra band, which performed every day from 2 p.m. to 12 a.m. at the bar of VIP International.

I switched on the television and tuned into a music channel playing an item number. I started dancing, matching steps with the sensuous girl in the song. As I was enjoying my drink and dance, I heard the doorbell ring.

"Hey Ghosh! Come on brother, it's nice to see you," I said.

"My pleasure, sir. Glad to get your *darshan*," he replied.

We gave each other a warm hug.

I offered Ghosh a drink.

"You never change, sir. Every time I see you, you look younger than before. How do you manage, sir?"

I smiled and said, "I let my inner child do the talking and keep my maturity inside."

We both laughed.

"Hey Ghosh! How's Nisha?" I asked.

"She left our band three months back and went to Mumbai to try her luck in Bollywood."

"Oh my God! What the fuck! She was the gem of your band and the queen of my heart," I said, placing my hand on my heart.

He laughed and said, "It's all your doing. You misled her to Bollywood."

"Me? How?"

"You praised her so much that her insane mind climbed to seventh heaven. She started behaving like a celebrity. You filled her with self-confidence and it fucked all of us," said Ghosh.

Ghosh seemed so livid that I burst into laughter.

"Look Ghosh, she was a real damsel. She was fascinating. She had talent. She does not belong here. Let her live her dream," I said and continued, "You know Ghosh, whenever she performed the *naagin* dance, my heart went hissing like a *naag* (snake). She was a charmer."

Ghosh laughed and said, "She was such a charmer that she even charmed Mr Charmer here."

We both laughed.

I saw Ghosh's empty glass and said, "Another drink!"

"If you get so drunk here, what will you do in the bar then? Let's move. It's only 6.45 p.m. now."

"I am not interested in going to the bar," I said, with a dull look on my face.

"Oh come on!"

Ghosh grabbed my hand and said, "There are many new girls. Annie is there. You like her too."

"Okay, wait a minute," I said.

I combed my long locks and put on my Ray-Ban Aviator night shades.

"Let's go," I said.

"Oho! You look like a film hero. Today, the girls will fall all over you," said Ghosh, looking at me.

I smiled and walked with him to the bar.

I entered the bar. I was impressed by the illusionary psychedelic environment. It was a delight to the eyes. The bar was houseful. The place was teeming with girls bathed under yellow and blue lights. The laser light effects made the ambience edgy and exciting. The people in the bar, on seeing me, gave me a special seat just in front of the stage. It was a white leather sofa. I sat in it and ordered my drink. The girls in the bar looked like divas, glowing under the shiny artificial lights and bright make-up.

I then saw Annie. Our eyes met.

"Hello," she whispered and offering her hand sweetly.

I shook her hand.

The band performed my favorite songs and dance numbers. I enjoyed myself and threw money generously. Envious eyes stared at me. But I did not care. I enjoyed myself thoroughly. I spent over two hours in the bar and then I called Ghosh.

"Okay Ghosh. Please excuse me now," I said.

"You are leaving? So early? You have a whole night ahead," said Ghosh.

"I am not feeling too well. Maybe I will come back after some time."

"Fine sir. As you wish."

I came to my room. It was 9.10 p.m. I was a little confused and didn't know what to do. I called Pandey.

"Hello Pandey *ji*. What are you doing?"

"Nothing sir. Just watching television with the kids."

"Come to my hotel."

"You have to go somewhere?"

"Just come. We will talk. Okay?" I said and disconnected the call.

I took a shower. It refreshed me. I ordered fish curry with rice, salad and the famous *rasgulla* for dessert. I made another drink for myself.

I was channel surfing and enjoying my drink when Pandey came in. So did my supper.

"Come Pandey *ji*. Sit here," I said, pointing towards the sofa.

The waiter served the food.

"Why you called me so late, sir? Any problem?" Pandey asked.

I offered him some food but he declined it.

"No sir. I am full," he said.

"Let's go for a long drive or anywhere you want to go."

"Sonaganchhi," he said, with a twinkle in his eyes.

"But I don't fuck prostitutes," I said.

"What's the difference, sir? They are girls too," he said casually.

"It's not about girls. It's about feelings. I mean there should either be love or lust between the girl and me. Not money. Money relates to work. And to me, sex is an art not an act. Do you understand?"

I didn't know what Pandey understood but he said, "Okay sir. Then we can watch a *mujra* or a cabaret show there."

"That sounds interesting. But can it be arranged?"

"Why not, sir? I know somebody there. Everything will be arranged."

I ate in a hurry as Pandey called someone on the phone.

"Hello Meenakshi. Hi, it's me. Pandey from Howrah."

I could not hear what was being said on the other end, but I could hear Pandey clearly.

"I am fine. Actually Meenakshi *ji*, a very special guest of mine wants to watch nude cabaret... Yes, yes *paisa wala babu hai*. Very nice man, a gentleman... I love you only, I want you. Okay, we are coming," said Pandey and disconnected the call.

He looked very happy. "Hurry sir. Work done. Let's do rock 'n' roll."

I loved the way he said 'rock 'n' roll.'

It took me twenty minutes to get dressed. It was 10.30 p.m. In the next ten minutes, we were literally flying on the quiet roads.

"So Pandey *ji*, I think you visit these places often," I teased him.

"What sir? I am also a human being. I have my physical needs. And you know my wife's illness. She is useless," he said in vexation.

"Don't say things like that. She is your wife. You married her. Do whatever you want to do, man. But being a human being, you must care for her, love her," I said.

Pandey kept quiet.

I then asked him, "Do you love the woman you were talking to?"

"I like her, sir."

"What kind of woman is she?"

"Oh! Very nice lady, sir. Almost fifty years old but she looks younger. She is a little fat, but hot. She came here when she was only thirteen. Now she is the boss of that building Dreamland. She is an emotional woman."

"That's good. But what is Dreamland?"

"Actually sir, Sonaganchhi is the largest red light area in Asia. There are more than 200 buildings here, very congested place. Every building has a name. Like Premagan, Premlagan, Wonderland, Blue Heaven, Raaslila and many more. Dreamland is one of them. There are all kinds of beautiful girls."

"What do you mean by all kinds?"

"Sir, it means Bengali, Nepali, Assami, North Indian, South Indian and even foreigners."

"Your general knowledge about Sonaganchhi is superb, Pandey *ji*," I teased him again.

"You are very funny, sir," he said and laughed.

We reached the place. Pandey parked the car near Dreamland.

A tout came towards us.

"Who is Pandey?" he asked.

"Me," Pandey replied.

"Come with me," he said

We walked behind him. He knocked on a door. A man opened the door.

"Come in," he said.

We went inside. It was the ground floor of a four-story building. We stood on the corridor of a straight gallery that divided the floor into two parts. Each part contained ten rooms in a row. There was a narrow spiral staircase near the corridor. The first room on the right belonged to the boss, Meenakshi Devi. There were girls standing outside the door of their respective rooms. They wore scanty clothes but a lot of make-up.

We entered Meenakshi's room.

"Oh Pandey, welcome," she said happily.

Pandey smiled. I was behind him.

She looked at me as she sat on the bed.

I went close to her and kissed her hand.

Her face turned pink as she blushed at my sudden gesture.

"Oh my God! Shri Krishna himself has come to us. Come sit here," she said quickly.

I sat beside her smiling.

She pinched my cheeks.

"Very innocent. He is so very young, Pandey," she said, beholding my face.

Pandey smiled and said, "Please arrange liquor for us."

"Okay Pandey," said Meenakshi. And then turning to me, she asked, "What do you drink, Krishna?"

I told her my favorite brand, while Pandey asked for beer.

She called for Munna and told him to get our drinks.

"And bring it fast. He is a very special guest," she yelled and turned to Pandey. "So Pandey *ji*, you came here after a long time. How's your life going?"

Pandey just smiled. Munna then came back with the drinks and snacks.

"You can go now, Munna," said Meenakshi.

As Munna turned to leave, I said in a hurry, "Please bring me a pack of Gold Flake. King size."

"Okay," Munna replied.

Pandey opened the bottle himself, while Meenakshi poured water into my glass.

"You are very beautiful, Meenakshi *ji*, outside as well as inside," I said very politely.

She looked at me in amazement. Her eyes were moist as she said, "First time in my life, I feel so proud to be a woman. Thank you very much, sweetheart." She then kissed my forehead.

By then Pandey had finished half the bottle of beer. I had taken just a sip.

"Look Pandey, learn something from him on how to treat a woman. He is so cute," said Meenakshi.

With alcohol tossing in his mind, Pandey said with envy, "What cute? He is thirty years old, very clever. You don't know anything about him. He is a powerful man, a *gunda*…"

"Shut up, Pandey," I yelled at him.

Pandey hesitated in fear. He kept quiet.

I gulped my drink in anger. I thought, "So this is what he thinks about me. What an idiot!"

Meenakshi looked at me in disbelief as though she had seen a ghost.

"No no, Pandey. This not right. He is really very cute. He is my Krishna," she said.

Pandey was silent.

"Where are the girls, Meenakshi *ji*?" I asked, to change the topic.

In five minutes, the room was crowded with girls. I looked at every girl. They were trying really very hard to impress me. Some even winked at me. It was as though the girl I chose would be crowned Miss Sonaganchhi.

Suddenly, a damsel caught my eyes. She was standing very calmly in a corner of the room, unaware of her fascinating beauty. Oh, she was different!

She was dressed in a white sleeveless V-neck linen *kurti* and a long black crepe skirt. She wore no make-up except collyrium in her eyes and a glossy pink lipstick. An emerald necklace and matching earrings increased her sex appeal. Curly locks fell on her collar bone casually. She had sharp facial features and a well-toned ripe body with stark curves. The Almighty had indeed blessed her with immense sensuality. Her skin was the color of the new moon.

I wondered who she was and how I could impress her. I closed my eyes and took a deep breath. I quickly finished my drink and lit a cigarette, ignoring everyone in the room. I took two deep puffs before crushing the cigarette with my shoe.

I looked at her as though there was no one else in the room. I penetrated her eyes quickly, faster than the speed of light. I wondered if what I felt was love or lust.

It is dangerous to jump into a silent river without knowing its depth. An unmeasured fall can cause severe pain. So it is better to first throw a stone into the river to gauge its depth.

Several thoughts gushed into my mind in a split second. I was ready to face the challenge. I slowly walked towards her. Our eyes met. I bent on my knees and held her hand. She was a little startled but managed to hide it well. Her eyes were wide open in amazement as she had not expected this. With compassionate eyes, I said in an intense voice, "I have seen many eyes, but yours are deep like an ocean. I have seen many faces, but yours is a lotus. I have seen many lips, but yours are like rose petals. I have seen many women, but you are an angel. You know sweetheart, I can spend my whole life with you. But may I have the pleasure of spending a night with you?"

"Okay," she said politely.

I drowned in her sonorous voice.

The girls clapped. Some even kissed me. A few girls wanted my mobile number. They forgot everything, they forgot their business.

"Go to your rooms, leave him alone," Meenakshi shouted, waking up to reality.

The girls left the room, talking among themselves about what had just happened.

"She is Mona," Meenakshi said.

I smiled. Meenakshi smiled too.

"Look Pandey, I told you that he is Krishna. First time in my life I saw so much love, so much happiness in their eyes. These emotionless prostitutes sleep with men only for money, but did you notice that they were all dying to sleep with him?"

She continued, "And Mona, you came here a year ago. He is the first person you have said 'yes' to."

Mona looked at me suspiciously.

I laughed and said, "It's not like that Meenakshi *ji*. Would you please show me my room, so that I can spend some time with Mona?"

"Why go to another room? Stay here. Pandey and I will leave. It's your room now. Enjoy," said Meenakshi.

I said nothing. Pandey and Mona looked at Meenakshi in surprise.

"Do you want anything else?" Meenakshi asked me.

"No thanks," I replied.

"Let's go, Pandey."

Pandey followed Meenakshi. I heard the door close.

I removed my shoes and lay down on the bed like a king resting on his throne.

"Neither do I know cabaret nor am I interested in sleeping with you," said Mona.

"Did I ask you to sleep with me? And yeah, I don't sleep with a harlot."

"Mind your language. I am not a prostitute."

"Then who are you?"

"I am a doctor and I am here for research."

"On what?"

"Men's sexual behavior."

"That's great. Would you please make me a drink?" I asked very gently.

She looked at me like a mother looked at her child. She did what I asked her to do.

"Do you drink?" I asked her.

"Yes, sometimes But I prefer vodka."

"What's the difference? The purpose is the same. Make yourself one."

She passed me my drink.

I kept the glass aside and made her a drink.

She said tauntingly, "So Mr Krishna, you are so young. You must concentrate on your studies and career rather than spending your parent's hard-earned money here. You seem to be from a nice family. Why are you getting wasted?"

"I love you. I want to know you," I said simply.

"Do you know what my age is? I am forty years old. And you are like my son. But if you want to fuck me, remove your clothes. Do it fast and get out of this place. You don't even know the meaning of love," said Mona, in anger.

"First of all, stop playing my mother or teacher. Okay? Secondly, do you know the meaning of love?"

"Love is pure. It is worship. It is total surrender," she replied.

"That's very nice. But have you ever experienced pure love? Have you ever loved anyone totally or worshipped anyone?"

"No," she said, a bit hesitant.

"Then your idea of love is bookish, it is imaginary. It means you don't know anything about love and you know why? Because you always doubted. You always questioned."

She looked earnest as I said this. She then turned pale.

Mona then asked me, "How old are you?"

"I am a just born baby," I said and laughed.

"What nonsense!"

"I am sorry, dear. I was just kidding. Actually, 'I am a just born baby' is the title of the novel I am writing," I said, hoping to pique her interest in me.

"So, you are a writer?"

"Not really. I mean, I have not yet written a book. I only have the concept. The book is incomplete now."

"Bullshit. I think you don't have any story. You just said that to impress me. Right? I know men's fucking game plan," she said.

She looked as though she really wanted to hit me hard. But actually her motive was to scratch the surface and unearth the truth.

I answered patiently, "That is not true, Mona. I will write this novel one day. And I don't want to impress you with lame jokes. I want to win your heart."

"Whatever! I am not interested. You did not answer my question."

"Which question?"

"How old are you?" she asked again.

"Thirty."

"What? You are lying," she said, a little startled.

"Why would I lie to you? Will it help me win your heart?"

"I can't believe it. I mean… Look at you. Your innocent eyes… That cute smile, your dressing, your physique. There is no sign of maturity except the words coming from your mouth. You know, I thought you were twenty."

My heart bounced a bit. Emotions were riding high inside me. If I pulled them out, they would perhaps start doing a hip-hop dance on the bed. So I controlled my emotions.

"Oh! So you observed me very carefully. It's my pleasure," I said gently.

"Of course. But you don't make any sense. What about you? You did not notice me?"

"Yes, from head to toe. You are very sexy," I said passionately.

"You guys are really impossible. You only see sex in women. Anyway, why are you trying so hard to impress me? You have paid for me, so please go on. Do whatever you want to do, man," she said furiously.

I kept calm and said, "I won't fuck you till you desire it."

"That will never happen. Stop dreaming. I know you people always lust for a woman's body. You are no saint. I know why you are here. Quench your thirst with my body like a vulture plucking flesh from the dead," she said rudely.

What she said hit me really hard this time. I was fuming.

"Did I even try to touch you? Did I look at you indecently? Did you see in my eyes hunger for your body, even for a single moment? Even if you lie down naked, I won't touch you. Okay?"

She looked down.

"What's the difference between a man and a woman or a girl and a boy? It's not the gender. Women are smart in everything but dumb in sex. You use love as a cover to hide your lust. And I have not come here as a hungry sex maniac or a high-headed rich kid. I have my purpose. I found you different and that's why I chose you. But you won't understand it. Leave it. I don't need your love," I yelled at her.

The raging fire in me melted her icy core. Her eyes were wet. But I ignored her completely. I quickly fixed a drink and gulped it in a hurry.

"I am leaving," I said and bent to pick up my shoes.

She grasped my hand.

"Please don't go. I am sorry," she said in an intense voice.

Her touch vaporized my anger.

I looked at her.

"Oh my God! What did I do?" I asked.

Tears fell from her eyes.

A tear drop was about to fall on her sharp-edged lip. I quickly moved and held the precious drop with my lips. She closed her eyes at my sudden gesture, as though she wanted to live in the moment forever. Suddenly, a flood of tears rained on my face, through the sieve of her eyelids. The mild fragrance of her breath intoxicated my mind. We were immersed in the fascinating moment.

"I don't want to bathe in your tears, okay?" I said, shattering the mirage.

She blushed and laughed, as she came out of her stupor.

"You are an impostor," she said sonorously.

"Oh. It's true. I am Krishna. Didn't you hear what Meenakshi *ji* said?"

I laughed, lightening the tense atmosphere a bit.

"Do you love me?" she asked me.

"Yes, from the bottom of my heart," I replied.

"But you don't even know me."

"I am always interested in knowing myself, not others. But since you asked, let me think of an answer. A single moment is enough to know someone. Or even a whole life may be insufficient. It is better to know yourself completely than know someone else. So the question is, do you know yourself?"

"Yes, I know myself," she insisted.

"No, you don't."

"How do you know that I don't know myself?"

"I pervade the internal parts of the universe. I am acquainted with the matters of the heart. I am Krishna. Sometimes, your belief becomes another person's faith."

"How do you know such things? You are so young. I mean, you look innocent, but you are wicked. You are also a jovial person. You are confusing."

I clapped softly.

"Thank you very much, dear. Anything else?" I asked, looking at her intently.

"You are fascinating and crafty too. Actually, you are magical," she said and laughed loudly.

"Your laughter enamors me," I said.

She put her head down in modesty. She was smiling mildly.

"To know the unknown, you must block your doubts and questions," I said.

"Okay. And how do I do it?"

"Acceptance. That's the only way."

"What?" she asked in confusion. "Are you kidding?"

"No. It's the truth. Look, it's very simple but sometimes the simple things are complicated."

"What does it mean? What you say is very confusing. Will you please clarify?"

"If you deny something, it means you are not accepting it. There is a purpose. If you accept something, nothing is there. The purpose vanishes. Love is the first thing we all deny. So the purpose always remains—to hate. Acceptance is the best denial."

I felt a little awkward. She was staring at me very sweetly as she dipped into my wisdom. I waved my hand in front of her eyes to break her reverie. Looking a little perplexed, she grabbed my hand and placed it on her navel.

"What?" she said smiling. It was a huge smile that tried to hide her attraction towards me.

"So, you want to do it now?" I asked, looking at her navel.

She removed my hand in hurry.

"Oh, you are impossible!" she blushed.

I laughed loudly.

"You know, actually I have never been so close to a man for fifteen long years. It's not that I don't like it. But the reasons are my hectic work, morality, family. The truth is it never happened or I did not care for it. That's why every time you do or say something, my heart flips for you. I feel silly, I behave silly. Yes, I am delighted. You have charmed me. And you know, acceptance is the best denial."

A naughty smile scattered across our faces. As our eyes met, the smile turned into laughter. We both had opened to each other. I quickly changed my expression from intense to relaxed, as I could not stay in one mood for long.

"By the way, what's your real name, Mr Krishna?"

"What's in a name?" I said, smiling and looking lovingly at her.

"It's my right to know the name of person who has charmed me, who has stolen my heart," she said, placing one hand on her heart. The act was childish, but she made it look elegant.

"Kunwar Nitin," I said and raised my glass of whisky.

"Nice name, showing your royalty," she whispered.

I did not care for royalty. I took a sip from the glass and said, "So Ms Mona, what's your real name?"

"What's in a name, Kunwar?" she said, imitating me.

I laughed mildly.

"As you wish. Anyway, I am not interested in names."

"So, Kunwar *ji*, what's your interest? Women?" she taunted me.

"Yes, of course. I love women. But right now my interest is your interest."

"What do you mean? What's my interest?" Mona asked suspiciously.

"People always forget the purpose," I said cunningly.

"Oh yes, I get it. Experiencing true love. To know the unknown," she said sarcastically.

I did not mind the sarcasm.

"So, are you willing?" I said.

"Yes, but how do we experience it? What is the right way?"

"Through our bodies…"

"What?" She seemed a little startled. "You mean intercourse?"

"Yes," I said and emptied the glass.

Suddenly, I laughed aloud.

She was embarrassed.

"Why are you laughing now?"

"Nothing! Just a thought that made me laugh."

"What thought? Tell me," she said impatiently.

"You are doing a PhD on this topic and you call it 'intercourse.'" I laughed sarcastically.

She laughed as well. "Very funny, Kunwar *ji*," she said, distorting her face to mock me. But I thought she was mocking herself than me.

I found her face alluring. So I stared at her face in fascination. There was silence for some time.

"You know, you are a sensualist," she said soberly, breaking the silence.

"I won't deny that. I accept everything. Acceptance helps me cleanse my soul."

"Whatever. You only talk, you don't perform," she said in distress.

"Did you just surrender? Did you just approach me?"

"What? Women don't approach," she said in modesty.

"And I don't approach them."

"But you said you love women. Right?"

"But I did not say that I approach them."

"What's the problem?"

"Look, men always approach women. That is common. But a woman approaching a man, that is rare. Rare, unusual things excite me."

"This is egotism, this is arrogance," she said, a little vexed.

I smiled while she continued acrimoniously.

"It means you fuck any woman who approaches you."

"Yes of course. But this is not about ego or arrogance or fucking. It's about purpose."

"And your purpose is to enjoy, right?"

I did not answer her directly. Instead, I posed a question. "Isn't that your purpose?"

"Yes. Everyone's purpose is to enjoy and reproduce. That's why we make love."

"Well, my purpose is joy, not enjoyment."

"What's the difference?"

"Huge difference. Enjoyment is limited, joy is infinite."

"You are confusing me."

"Listen, I don't approach a woman because I want to enjoy. But when a woman approaches me, it gives me a purpose. I find her lustful and desirous. She really wants it badly. I became more sensual, more amorous. And I use all the lust, passion and desire towards an orgasm. I create real joy and awakening. I only care for her joy. I only care for her orgasm. I only care for her awakening. I only care about what the woman gets. I love women. So there is no point in me approaching women. Besides, it would be really ridiculous if I approach a woman and say, 'Hey come on, I wanna give you an orgasm.' The point is what does she want? What does she need? I don't need to enjoy as I am filled with joy."

Mona hugged me in extreme pleasure. Incited, she caressed my face.

"I am all yours. I surrender to you," she whispered into my ear.

My words had obviously melted her heart.

I gently detached her from my body. Removing my hand softly from her head, I asked, "How does it feel?"

She burst into tears.

"Save me Kunwar. I am suffering. I am a sinner. I am unworthy."

I was stunned.

I swiftly held her tight between my arms.

Her intense uproar reduced me to nothing. I caressed her back with my hands. My act helped calm her.

"I am sorry, Kunwar," she said in a shaky voice.

She tried to gather herself as she looked down.

"Don't worry, dear. It's okay," I said lovingly and lifted her face.

As our eyes met, our lips too entangled with each other for a while.

"What's the matter? What happened to you?" I asked.

"It's a long story, Kunwar. A burden of my past. A burden on my filthy body. A burden on my soul. It haunts me each and every moment. There is only darkness inside," she said in an intense voice.

"I am listening to you. I want to hear your story. Share your burden, set yourself free."

"Not now. Wait. I want my orgasm. I want to be awakened. I want joy. Can't you see the effect of your enchantment? I am burning, Kunwar. You have stimulated my inactive emotions. I am a lustful woman now. Quench my thirst. Release me from my own bonds."

She spoke so passionately as her eyes brimmed with wetness. I held her hands and kissed them gently.

Then I said, "Okay, but I have two questions."

"Ask them."

"Can you walk like a wild cat?"

She knew what I meant and said, "Yes. You want me to shed my inhibitions."

"Yes. But I want you to first accept that you are a wild cat. It helps release yourself from your hesitations, your burden. It frees your body and body language. It shortens time and distance."

Mona posed like a wild cat and produced a growling sound.

I laughed loudly. "Don't act, just accept."

She laughed too. "What is your next question?" she asked eagerly.

"Do you know your G-spot?"

"I have heard of it but I don't really know the exact location. I mean, who cares? If it is there, let it be there. After all, everything gets crushed when the mortar is pounded," she said, candidly and innocently at the same time. I laughed.

"Your G-spot is the point of your orgasm. It's the most sensitive source point. We have to find it."

"But how?" she asked, in anxiety.

"Wait a minute." I picked up my mobile phone and put it on silent mode.

I then placed the phone on one corner of the bed. It was 3 a.m.

I said, "Well, we have to find it practically."

I instructed her about the method. She listened sincerely. As she went ahead with the two-finger test, she was quivering in excitement. She lay down on the bed on her back. She was in an intense, heated state. I was between her folded legs.

I kissed her sacred source sensually. She swiftly jolted her body and groaned in pleasure as she felt the deep sensation caused by my lips.

She looked tempting. I leaped on her ripe body. Our bodies fused together in intoxication. We were in sync, physically and mentally. She could read my thoughts, she could sense my senses.

After some topsy-turvy moments and an intense, intimate session of foreplay, Mona posed like a wild cat. Careless, shameless, naked. I pretended to ride her like a cavalier.

"Nitambini (a woman with beautiful buttocks)," I whispered.

As I engrafted the tip of my source into the opening of her source, we could feel the heat of a crater. She hissed. This was followed by a round of pounding, as she raised her body towards my chest to embrace me. She was very flexible even at her age. She impressed me.

I tightened her between my arms. We were very close, as our palpitation matched steps. I was drunk with ecstasy in the scent of her body. Our breaths quivered together harmoniously. So did our bodies. Her melodious billowing was exciting. It was an extremely amorous state to be in. The pounding made way for rubbing, as we were glued together. We were going with the flow of our bodies. The physical act of intercourse became an art. Very intimate, very intense.

As I had instructed her to concentrate only on my breathing, she was focused only on it. Our breathing was interwoven. I concentrated on her G-spot. Biologically and technically, we were into each other. We were dissolving. We were breathing heavily. We dissolved. We immersed into each other. This time, it was real.

There was deep silence as we both fell into an infinite, dark and vacant space. It was a very sharp fall. It was so acute, that we shrank our bodies. We closed our eyes in fear. We were balanced. We were floating. There was nothing else, except us. Suddenly, we saw two bright dots moving very fast, energetically and violently towards each other, along the same path. As they collided, they exploded, dispersing a huge amount of energy all over the ample space—in the form of a milky-white light. The light is our vision now. Range of eye sight became infinite. We became far-sighted.

We were still active physically. She was billowing in delight. Each thrust pleased her immensely. She was shaking her buttocks ardently, as she badly wanted to be entwined in me. At the same time, she was somewhere else. She was in nothing but light. She had foresight. She was crossing to Milky Way. As she emerged, at the other side of ample light. she wondered in delight. She was amazed with the creation all around her. Everything seemed unusual. There was day and night at the same time. It seemed like dawn. But then, there was the dark blue sky with twinkling stars. How was it possible?

She thought. She observed carefully. The place was surrounded by snow-covered mountains. There was greenery all over the ground. Peacocks danced in illusion to a melodious tune from an unknown source. Embers were falling from the sky but when they touched the ground, they turned into golden butterflies. It was wonderful. The continuous fall of embers caused hanging shutter of flickering lights. At the end of her vision, she saw an ellipse of bright light. The mountains ended there. There was a rainbow colored waterfall from a great height. Then there was an arched gateway of floating white jasmine flowers. The hanging gateways formed a floral gallery, which ended at the waterfall. The weather was very charming. The air was vital and aromatic. It was a wonderland. It was heaven.

She whispered. And then she started walking like a cat. Oh my God! She looked like a celestial damsel walking naked. Her body glittered. A golden butterfly came flying and embraced her. It stuck its wings beneath her collarbone above her heart, giving the impression of a live tattoo. Wow! She was a fairy to die for. Her each step was rhetorical. Physically, we were approaching climax. I was caressing her gently and she was screaming in intense pleasure. It was echoing throughout the room. As she reached the end of the gallery, following an attractive and melodious tune, she drowned in the aroma of the flowers. She was wonderstruck.

It was incredible. It was like a rainbow lake, a rainbowfall. She was excited. She was in joy.

"This is an ambrosia." "This is a nectar." Drink it, she heard an intense melodious heavenly voice. She scooped a handful of the nectar and brought it close to her mouth.

There was a dense flame of rainbow as her eyes opened wide in amazement. She tilted her neck upward and drank the nectar. She was filled with illusionary delight. As she drank the nectar, the rainbowfall turned into a hanging rainbow of stairs. She rushed to climb the stairs. Her excitement increased with every step. As she neared the top, she was blushing with joy. Finally, she reached the top. She was at the zenith of joy. She laughed insanely. She swung in pleasure. Rose petals fell from the sky covering her naked body like a fancy gown. She felt a thrilling sensation.

Physically, we were on the top of climax.she roared in joy as she experienced multiple orgasms.I was shaking her with my violent jerks.

In her joy, she forgot the melody. As she came back to her senses, she glanced at me. She saw me. I was standing below the *kalpadruma* (the tree of paradise). I was playing my flute, naked. The platform of rainbow light ended in an ellipse. I was at the end. Between us were many naked couples dancing and swinging together, drowned in each other. The male form was the same in all the couples, while there were different female forms.

"Oh, this is the abode of Shri Krishna. This is his *raaslila*," she thought.

Deep in her thought, she walked towards me.

"So Kunwar, you are Krishna," she said enthusiastically. I could see the goosebumps on her skin.

I smiled. "I am Krishna, but I am not Kunwar," I said. "The face is an illusion. But I am real. I am your conscience. I am your soul. I am you."

"But how is it possible?" she asked, a little confused.

"Look, I am an interim and ultimate source. Everything is my expansion. I am constant, but my expansion changes. I am the origin. I am everywhere. In every change. In everything. Love is my expansion. My face is your love. I am inside this love. Your face is my love. I am inside this love. So, love remains the same, only the face changes. The face is the expansion of love, so it changes. Love is the soul and I am its essence."

"So, I am a soul," she said.

I laughed. "You are peering into your soul now. Look in front of you, your soul is making merry with your love."

As she looked around, she was wonderstruck again.

This time, the female form was the same in all the couples. But the male was different.

We were dancing, drowned in each other. She was the female in every couple.

"Oh my God," she whispered.

I laughed again. "This is what my *raaslila* is all about. I am Krishna. I am love. I am the highest happiness. I am your entity. Go now. It's time to play my flute," I said, very lovingly.

"Wait, wait, wait," she screamed in a hurry. "Do you know my deeds? Am I sinful? What will happen to me?" she asked

"As I am your conscience, I know everything. I know your past, I know your present, but I only have a glimpse of your future. You don't worry. Nothing is right or wrong. Nobody is pure or sinful. Everything happens for a reason. And the reason is change. Be the reason to change. Accept the reason of change. Love the change. Accept the love. I am always here with you. It is you who changes, so move with the changes," I said and started blowing my flute.

She closed her eyes in joy. The melody of the flute filled her with compassion. Tears came streaming out of her eyes like real grace falling from inside her. The grace of wisdom. She knew nothing was permanent and everything changed. She was happy and filled with the right and positive emotions.

We danced with joy. We drowned in each other. Everything vanished. There was light falling within. We were swinging rapidly. We turned into a curved mass of light. Due to our excessive and rapid swinging, the mass of light broke into two, expending a huge amount of energy. The two pieces were falling apart. As the distance between the pieces increased, they became small. Very small, tiny. Soon they became two dots. And finally, they dissolved in their respective infinite, dark vacuum space.

She was crying compassionately in joy. I was gasping as I was about to pour fluid into her source. She was in great intoxication of physical and heavenly delight. As we achieved our final emancipation, we fell on the bed in indolence. Our eyes were closed. I was breathing deep and palpitating fast. There was deep silence inside and outside.

I looked at her thoroughly. She looked like a girl who had just attained freedom. I could see the pores on her skin clearly. A drop of sweat declined at a wet curve, as it eagerly waited to fill her ripened body. She glowed like a new moon. Drops of joy fell in a row through her sharp-edged eyes and slipped into her dense wild hair. Her body imparted a musk fragrance all over.

"You are a real damsel," I whispered.

She opened her eyes, which were full of veins.

Looking at me affectionately and smiling in delight, she threw her arms round my neck, pulled me and embroidered my face with mild kisses.

"Thank you very much, Kunwar. It was an awesome experience. It was priceless," she said tenderly.

I held her hands and kissed them.

"It's my pleasure, darling."

I winked at her.

She laughed mildly.

"Why am I so wet? Why is this bedsheet so wet all over?" she asked, a bit anxiously, as she felt the dampness all around her.

"You squirted."

"What?" Now she was a little startled.

"Yes, at least fifteen times."

"Oh my God!"

She covered her face with her hands in shame. But she was laughing.

Composing herself, she said, "Oh Kunwar, this was an orgasmic orgasm. I have never felt anything like this in my whole life. You are awesome, you are my love, my love forever. You are Krishna."

And then she smooched me in great delight.

As we detached, I requested her to make me a drink. Pouring the liqueur into a glass, she asked me, "Why do you drink so much? It's harmful."

"Not for me. It cures me," I said and laughed a little.

"You are charming and you are always charmed," she said, passing me the drink.

She smiled. I saw the time. It was 4.45 a.m. I calculated. "We had been in coitus for an hour and fifteen minutes."

"Really?" she asked, a bit amazed. "I mean, it's a long time. I must be exhausted. But I am feeling nice. Very fresh and free. Like nothing has happened."

I smiled. I quenched my thirst with the drink.

"You have guts, man," she said, in an intense voice.

"Oh. That means you earlier doubted my guts," I said, a bit displeased.

"It's not my fault. It's yours. You made me have doubts. You are an impostor. I told you before."

"How?" I asked, finishing my drink.

"It's your outlook, it's your personality. You look like a careless brat. Very jovial, very *filmi*. You don't look strong, you look cute. You don't look like a thirty-year-old man. You look like a boy who loves to hover around teenage girls. You look immature. But from inside, you are dense, compassionate, mature enough to fuck maturely. You are sensitive and mighty. Overall, you are glorious inside."

"Really? Now you know a lot about me."

I winked as her words delighted me.

"You know, if I had met you somewhere outside, I would have rejected you for sure," she teased me.

I made a weepy face.

"You are a girl's material, not a woman's interest," she continued teasing me.

"Whatever! Leave it. I don't want to talk to you."

I then glued my eyes to the mobile phone screen.

She clasped my hand and said politely, "I was just kidding, dear."

"I don't care," I said and detached her hand from mine.

I continued playing with my phone.

"You don't know what you have done to me," she said, in an intense voice.

"What?" I asked eagerly.

"My past brought disgrace to me. But you filled me with grace. You filled me with wisdom. Now I am free. Free from all bondage. I am a graceful woman now," she said, with thankful eyes. Her eyes were wet.

I laughed. She lovingly slapped me.

"Tell me about your past. I want to hear your story," I said.

"Okay, but can I ask you something?"

"Sure."

"Was everything real, during our lovemaking? Whatever I experienced, whatever I saw… The *raaslila*, the nectar and all those things. Do they exist?"

"Look, everything you saw was real but they were your illusion. Like everything in this room is real but an illusion."

"You mean, my conscience, my soul, Krishna? Right?"

"Yes,"

"But didn't Krishna exist on earth long time ago, during the Mahabharata period?"

"Does it matter now? Listen, everything is a creation. And creation always exists. So, Krishna exists. But the real Krishna was the one who created the Krishna illusion. Got it? Now, stop fucking my mind. Tell me your story."

"Okay, okay, okay," she said hurriedly. "One last question, please," she said sweetly.

"Ask."

"How do you know all these things?"

"Come here."

She came close to me.

I whispered something in her ear. As I finished, she started laughing madly. She clapped her hands and said, "You are impossible. Promise me you won't tell anybody this."

Our eyes met and we burst into laughter.

Chapter - 2

WOUNDED

My real name is Mimosa Chatterjee. I belong to Kolkata. My father was a chef in a five-star hotel in San Francisco. So my family settled in San Francisco when I was just ten years old.

After my schooling, I met Dhruva Khanna. He was my neighbor and college mate. We both liked each other a lot. This soon turned into love and we decided to get married. We got married when I was only nineteen; he was twenty-four. After a year, I gave birth to a baby boy. We named him Coral. We were very happy.

Time passed smoothly and happily. I became a famous cosmetic surgeon in San Francisco. When I was not busy giving girls, models and wealthy women the perfect makeover with great boobs and butts, I took care of my son who was ten years old. Dhruva chipped in with the chores. Everything was perfect.

But one day, grief knocked on my door.

Dhruva died of a sudden and severe heart attack. I was senseless for two days. But gradually, I composed myself for the sake of my beloved son, Coral.

I was alone as my parents had gone back to Kolkata after the birth of Coral.

But time was the healer. We were soon back on track.

Nine years later, one day when I was in my clinic, my phone rang.

"Hello, Mimosa. It's Dhruva's uncle from Chandigarh."

"Oh, hello uncle. *Namaste*. How are you?"

"I am fine. But I have bad news for you."

"What's the news, uncle? Do tell me. I am very strong now."

"Your father-in-law is no more."

"Oh!"

There was silence for about thirty seconds.

"He wanted his last rites to be performed by his grandson Coral," said uncle, breaking the silence.

"But you know uncle, it's not possible to come to India at such a short notice. And I have to talk to Coral too. You know this generation, and there is my work too," I replied.

"Yes, it's right. Okay. Don't worry about the funeral rites. It will be done."

"Thank you very much, uncle."

"It's all right. Yes, one more thing, he made Coral his successor in his will."

"What? I don't understand."

"It means Coral is now the owner of his grandfather's property, which includes two acres of land in Chandigarh district, a flat in a posh society of Gurgaon that almost costs a crore and a showroom in Connaught Place in New Delhi."

"Oh my God! Really?"

"Yes, and you must think about settling in India. What is there in San Francisco? You are alone there. We all miss you."

"You are right, uncle. But you know my job is like that I don't think I have any scope in India."

"Oh my God! What are you saying? India has changed now; it is not less than America in any manner. Even your aunty wants her figure to be like a film actress' figure," he said and laughed.

I laughed too.

"Okay, uncle. But give me some time."

"Yes Mimosa, take your time. But my suggestion is come back to India. There are good opportunities for you and your son here. Think about it."

"Sure uncle. But excuse me now, I have a client waiting. I will call you tomorrow."

"Okay, *beti*, God bless you," he said and disconnected the call.

After finishing with my client, I came home. I took a shower as I was exhausted after dealing with many clients. I made a cup of coffee, leaned back on the sofa and thought, "Uncle is right. Here I am alone. Nobody is here to look after us. If anything happens to me, who will care for Coral? At least in India he has a certain future and family members to look after him.

His paternal lineage is his real privilege. We must go to India. I will talk to Coral."

I finished my coffee and searched on Google about the scope of my work in India. And I was surprised to find so many changes in my country. I hadn't bothered to keep track of the changes for twenty-six years. How could I detach myself from the current affairs in India? How could I have been so stupid?

I switched on the TV and watched a few Indian channels on news, music and entertainment. I checked the time. It was 6.45 p.m.

"Oh, it's time to work out," I whispered. I was a fitness freak and loved my body. I did not like to go under the knife to be in shape. So I dedicated thirty minutes in the morning and evening every day for a workout.

After my workout, I was relaxing when Coral came to me.

"Hi mom," he said.

"Hi son," I replied.

He was smiling. I loved his smile. It meant everything to me.

"You look damn hot, more than my girlfriends," he said.

"Oh, really? Thank you very much dear, and you are my beloved son, my sweetheart. How was your day?"

"It was cool. I enjoyed a lot with my friend."

"That's great. Do you want anything?"

"No mom," he said and switched on the TV and tuned into an English music channel.

"Hey, I have news for you Coral."

"What mom?"

I told him about the conversation with uncle.

I thought he would rebel but he was very excited and happy.

"OMG, I love you, mom," he said and kissed me.

Though I was a little surprised, I was happy.

"I can't believe it. I am the owner of so much property," said Coral.

"It means you want to go to India?"

"Yes mom, why not?"

"Thank God! I was anxious about you. But now it is all right. I will talk to uncle tomorrow."

"Okay dear Mimosa," said Coral and hugged me.

The next day, I called Dhruva's uncle.

"Hello uncle. *Namaste*."

"Hello Mimosa. God bless you."

"We are coming to India."

"Oh, really? That's great news."

"Yes uncle. You know Coral is more excited than me."

He laughed. "And why not? He is our blood. So, when are you coming?"

"Next month, most probably."

"Okay, we are very happy. You have made a good decision."

"Thanks uncle. And convey my regards to aunty."

"Yes yes, Mimosa. Sure."

"*Namaste* uncle."

The call disconnected.

Coral had been listening to our conversation. He was happy.

"But mom, I have to leave behind my friends here."

"That's true, dear."

"Whatever. I will make new friends there."

"Oh, my son is so very intelligent," I said lovingly and kissed his forehead.

Coral hugged me.

After three months, we landed in India.

Uncle came to receive us at the Indira Gandhi International Airport in New Delhi. Coral was very happy to meet his dad's uncle.

We moved into our luxurious three-bedroom flat. We threw a small party for our relatives and society members after a week. Though people in Delhi were social, they were showy. Gradually, we adapted to the neighborhood. Though it was easy for me, it was a little difficult for Coral. But he somehow managed. In just six months, he became a perfect Haryanawi brat. He looked just like his father.

I joined the kitty party group of our society. My cosmetic surgeon job too ran successfully thanks to advertisements in newspapers and social media publicity.

It was Sunday. We were having breakfast. I said to Coral, "So dear, you are having a lot of fun now. What about your studies?"

"What about it, mom?"

"I mean, do you want to join any coaching institute for medical selection?"

"I don't want to be a doctor."

"But why? What's the problem?'

"I want to be a businessman, like my grandfather."

"But complete your education first."

"Mom, I am not interested in studies anymore. And please don't pressurize me. It won't work. I have decided. I will reopen my grandfather's showroom."

I tried my best to make him understand the importance of medical education but he wouldn't listen. He insisted on starting his business soon. Finally, he won.

"Okay, Coral. As you wish. But at least apply for a graduate course."

"Thank you very much, mom. I love you," he said quickly and embraced me.

After a month, Coral opened his grandfather's showroom retailing women's apparel and accessories at Connaught Place. He also applied to a correspondence course at the Delhi University. Several friends and relatives were present on the day of the showroom opening to wish him luck. Coral was very happy.

Soon we both got busy with our lives. One day, I called Coral from my clinic. It was 7 p.m.

"Hello Coral."

"Yes mom. Tell me."

"I will be an hour late today. Busy with a client. Okay?"

Okay mom. But make it fast, as we have planned to go to a disc today."

"Okay son, I will try my best."

I disconnected the call. I finished up with my client in a hurry and went home. As my clinic was very close to our flat, it took just ten minutes to reach home. I rang the bell. The maid opened the door.

"Where is Coral?" I asked.

"He is in the bedroom with Sheetal," the maid replied.

Sheetal was a class twelve student of Delhi Public School and the daughter of our neighbor Mrs Saxena.

I walked to Coral's bedroom. Sheetal and Coral were kissing each other. I cleared my throat.

"Oh mom, you came so early. How am I looking?" Coral asked.

"Oh Coral, you are looking damn handsome," I said.

Coral was a very good-looking guy. Well-built, tall and fair.

"Thanks mom," he said and hugged me.

"Hello aunty," Sheetal wished me.

"Hello Sheetal, you are looking pretty," I said.

"Thanks aunty," Sheetal said in delight.

"You guys are going alone to the disc or with some friends?" I asked.

"Actually mom, we are going with our friends. Including us, totally nine from this society," said Coral.

"That's great. So go now and enjoy," I said.

"But mom, we will come back late at night. So I have taken the other key with me."

"Very sensible, dear. That's why I love you so much, my son. Go now. It's almost 9 p.m.," I said.

Coral and Sheetal left.

I undressed and took a shower.

"What's for dinner?" I asked the maid, as I relaxed on the sofa.

"Fish curry and *chapatti*, madam," she answered.

"Wow, bring it fast. I am hungry," I said and switched on the TV.

Just then my mobile vibrated. It was a message from our kitty party group. I read it.

"Dear Mimosa, we have arranged a get-together outside the society at Café-Coffee Day tomorrow from 3 p.m. to 5 p.m. Regards, Archana Kapoor."

"This is a good idea. It will be fun," I thought.

I finished my supper. I watched some news and then went to my bedroom, as I felt very sleepy. I dreamt that Dhruva was making love to me. I enjoyed the dream completely.

Sometimes, I felt the need to meet new men and get intimate with them but I put my needs away due to Coral. I didn't want Coral to mistake me and think bad of me.

I woke up at 5.30 a.m. as usual. Stretching my muscles, I got up. Coral was sleeping. I made a cup of black coffee for myself.

"Good morning, madam," said the maid.

"Good morning, Minu," I said.

Minu smiled and then got busy with the household chores.

I walked towards the lift. I pressed '0.' We were on the 14th floor.

I was running to the society gym when I heard a voice.

"Hey Mimosa."

I turned back.

"Oh Mrs Gupta, good morning."

She came towards me.

"Oh my God, Mimosa. You look like Coral's elder sister. How do you manage?"

"It's all God's grace and my hard work."

"You are a budding youth," she said and laughed.

I laughed too.

"Hey Mimosa. Can you fix them?" she asked quietly, pointing towards her sagging but fleshy breast.

I laughed and said, "Yes I can. But did Mr Gupta tell you something?"

I teased her.

"Oh no. He doesn't even look at me. He is very mean. He has interest only in young girls now. But he doesn't realize he looks like a monkey himself," she said anxiously.

I laughed again.

"Don't worry, Mrs Gupta. That's why I am here. Your problem will be solved," I said in jest.

We both laughed.

Four days later, I was relaxing on the couch at home. I had come home early that day. Coral came in looking very happy.

"What happened dear?" I asked him.

"Oh mom, I am so happy today. I can't tell you how much."

"I know. Your face is saying everything. What's the matter?" I said lovingly.

"Oh mom, she was a bomb."

"Who was a bomb?"

"Today a girl came to my shop. Her name is Trishna. She is awesome, mom. She took my heart away."

"Did she explode on you?" I said and laughed.

"What rubbish!"

"You said that she was a bomb."

I laughed again.

"I am falling for her and you are making fun of me."

"What about Sheetal then? She is your girlfriend, right?"

"We are just passing time, and I can manage two girlfriends."

"What? When your dad and I met, love happened and we got married."

"That was the Nineties, mom. It is now the 21st century. Now, we love, fuck and forget the bitch."

"Oh my God! You guys are so rude. At least respect the girls."

Coral laughed.

"My innocent mom! Nowadays, if a boy respects a girl, the girl kicks the boy's ass and moves on with another one."

"Really? How weak is my general knowledge!" I said and laughed.

Coral laughed too.

Thus began Coral's love story. Coral and Trishna started dating. Coral tried to impress Trishna with costly gifts. They hovered around malls, multiplexes, parks and coffee lounges. Everywhere. Coral was delighted to be with Trishna. But it did not last long. Not even a month.

One day, when I got back home from office, I saw him drinking beer. He looked miserable.

"What happened, son?" I asked anxiously.

"Nothing, just leave me alone," he said.

I touched his cheeks very gently with my fingers.

"Please tell me, dear. Is everything okay?"

"That bitch fucked me."

"What do you mean?"

"Trishna ditched me mom."

I could clearly hear the hissing of his breath. He was seething inside like charcoal.

"Relax son, please. Don't worry. Everything will be all right."

"Nothing will be right now. I will teach her a lesson."

"Okay. But will you please explain everything to me?"

"Today, I went to Delhi University to meet Trishna. There she introduced me to her boyfriend. I was shocked. She used me, mom. My friends were right. I should have just fucked her and left her."

"Did she ever tell you ever that she loved you?"

"No, she didn't. Does it matter?"

"Maybe she saw you as a friend."

I managed to calm him down and make him understand the situation. Coral relaxed a bit.

"Forget her. You have Sheetal."

"I have Mimosa too," he said and laughed.

I laughed too and hugged him.

"Let bygones be bygones. Hey Coral. I have to tell you something."

"What mom?"

"Tomorrow I am going to Mumbai. My colleague Dr Sukrna needs my help on a case. So you have to drop me at the airport."

"Okay mom. I will drop you. What time?"

"Tomorrow at 10.30 a.m."

"Oh I will miss you, mom."

"I'll miss you too, dear."

We hugged again.

***

I reached Mumbai. Dr Sukrna introduced me to his client. She was a model.

"Hi Mimosa," she said.

"Hi," I replied. "So, what's your need?"

"Actually Mimosa, I am doing a film. But my director said that my lips are very flat. He wants my lips to be pulpy. You know, so that they look better when I pout."

"Okay. I got it. But it will take a few sessions."

"That's okay. No problem."

After completing the first session with the model, I asked Dr Sukrna, "Is there any nice hotel near your clinic?"

"What are you saying? Are you mad? You are coming with me to my house. My wife and my daughter will be very happy to meet you."

I wanted to stay in a hotel but he insisted on staying with him and his family. So I went to his house.

"She is my wife Durgabha and she is my daughter Matangi," Dr Sukrna introduced me to his family.

"Hello, I am Mimosa."

"You are my dad's student, right?" asked Matangi.

Dr Sukrna laughed aloud.

"She was my fellow student in college," he said.

"OMG! You look like my elder sister," said Matangi.

We all laughed.

Matangi was a very sweet and well-behaved girl. She was pursuing a course in fashion designing from the National Institute of Fashion Technology. I thought Coral and Matangi would be perfect together. Thinking so, I looked at my watch. It was 10 p.m. I called Coral but he did not answer my call. A little later, I got a message from him. "Mom, I am in a disc. Talk to you later. Love you. Bye."

"Love you too, sweetheart," I whispered.

I was so exhausted that I went into deep sleep the minute my head touched the pillow.

The next day, Dr Sukrna and I reached the clinic early. I called Coral again but his mobile phone was switched off.

I thought perhaps he was still sleeping. I switched off my mobile phone as I didn't want to be disturbed during work.

It was 5.30 p.m. The second session of the treatment came to an end. I showed the model a mirror.

"How does it look?" I asked her.

"Wow, it's nice. The color is perfect, but I can't feel them. And what about the swelling?"

"It will take some time, but don't worry."

Then I instructed her on a few precautions.

"Thanks Mimosa."

I switched on my mobile phone. There were thirty missed calls and an SMS. All from uncle. The message said, "Call me, it's very urgent."

I called him. "Hello uncle. What's the matter?"

"Come back to Delhi as soon as you can. Hurry."

"What happened? Is everything all right?"

"The police arrested Coral this morning. Come soon."

A strange kind of fear gripped my mind. My heart was palpitating fast.

"Okay uncle," I said and disconnected the call.

Dr Sukrna booked me on a flight immediately.

I was blank.

Uncle came to the airport to receive me.

"What did he do, uncle?"

"Some girl name Trishna accused him and his friends of raping her."

"Oh my God! That's horrible. Where is she?"

I was shivering.

"She has been hospitalized as they apparently beat her up barbarically while raping her."

"What will happen to Coral now? Uncle, he is my only son."

I was crying.

"Don't worry, Mimosa. Nothing will happen to Coral."

"We will use all our powers to save him. I have called my lawyer. He will meet us at the police station," uncle said firmly.

His words comforted me, but I was still concerned about Coral.

"How is he managing in the filthy lock-up?" I muttered to myself anxiously.

Uncle heard it.

"Oh don't worry. The sub-inspector there is known to me. He is taking care of him."

We reached the Connaught Place police station where we met Abhimanyu Dubey, our lawyer.

"We can't get a bail now, as it's a very sensitive matter and a case of the fast-track court," said the lawyer.

"Can I meet him?" I asked

"Oh sure," he said.

We walked up to the lock-up. I was shivering and my heart was palpitating fast yet again.

Coral was behind bars with his friends. They look like wicked loafers.

"What did you do, son?" I said. Tears filled my eyes.

"Oh nothing, mom. Don't worry, my friends are very influential. Nothing will happen," he said. He seemed relaxed.

"But how did it happen? I told you to forget her."

"When you went to Mumbai, I called her. She came to meet me. At 8 p.m., we went to a lounge in Gurgaon. There we met my friends. We were all drunk. She too enjoyed herself. Under intoxication, I tried to kiss her. She slapped me in front of the whole crowd and rushed to the parking lot. I walked behind her, and so did my friends. I was behaving nicely to her but she abused me. It then became unbearable. I taught her a lesson. We fucked her one by one. She provoked me, mom."

"Why did you beat her so brutally? You don't have any humanity in you?" I asked him, pretending to be angry.

"She was resisting, mom, she was fighting. Look, she scratched my face. She gave us no choice."

"You are an idiot, Coral. If you had not beaten her, she certainly would not have told anybody about the rape. You left her badly bruised. And so she gained lot of sympathy and sympathizers," I rebuked him.

"Leave it now, Mimosa," uncle interrupted. "He is young and we all have done such mistakes in our youth. We should focus on getting him released. We have to bring him out clean, at any cost."

"Excuse me, sir," said the sub-inspector.

"Oh, Mr Tomar, please tell us," said uncle.

"Actually sir, you go home. I will take care of him. Any time, circle officer will drop in on reporting. He is an honest person."

"Okay and thank you very much," said uncle and gave him an envelope. He silently kept the envelope in his lower pocket.

"Let's go, Mimosa," said uncle.

I didn't want to go but there was no other option. I left with uncle and the lawyer.

After the first hearing of the case, our lawyer told us, "Look everybody, we are going to lose this case."

"What?" we asked together. Uncle and I were shocked.

"What are you doing then? We have paid you enough," said uncle.

I was about to faint but I gathered myself. I was crying.

"What can I do? Her case is very strong. She has many witnesses who saw Coral and Trishna together that night. And the doctor has confirmed her rape in court."

"Oh my God, please save my son Mr Dubey," I cried. I implored earnestly.

"Is there no way to save Coral?" uncle asked the lawyer in disappointment.

"There is a way. That's why I called you. And it's the only way to save your child," the lawyer announced.

"Please explain. We can do anything," said uncle.

We were both anxious.

"If Trishna withdraws her charges against the guys or if she dies before the final hearing...," said the lawyer.

"Are you crazy? Why would she withdraw her charges? Is it possible?" asked uncle.

"Everything is possible. Offer her a huge compensation, which she can't refuse."

Uncle and I agreed to this suggestion. We valued her dignity at one crore rupees.

Dubey was cunning and sharp. He had gathered a lot of information about Trishna and her family. He said, "Look, Trishna is a small town girl and belongs to a lower middle class family. Hers is a small family of four with her mother, father and a ten-year-old younger brother. Her father is a bank clerk. So one crore is an appropriate and solicitous amount to her family."

It was decided that I would visit Trishna in the hospital. Since I was a woman and a doctor too, it was not hard for me to get access to Trishna's room in the hospital.

It was 10.30 p.m. There was deep silence in the room. The silence of grief.

Trishna was reposed against a folding bed and her mother was feeding her with a spoon very lovingly. Her father was reading a book in a corner.

Trishna's swollen and trampled face was a harsh indicator of the demonic behavior of the boys.

"*Namaste*, I am Coral's mother," I said to Trishna's father.

They looked at me in shock.

"Look what your son did to my daughter. Why did you come here? To sprinkle salt on our wounds?" Trishna's mother yelled at me.

I was crying.

"Please forgive my son. I can't return the dignity of your daughter, but you can give me back my son's life. I am begging you. Please show some mercy," I cried and gave her mother a check for one crore.

Trishna's mother lit up on seeing it.

Seeing her interest in the money, I continued, "What you will get from all these litigations, except bad name? Who will marry your daughter? What will be the future of your only son? This is a huge amount. You can make your future, as you wish. But please help me release my only son."

Trishna's father interrupted. "Don't take it."

"Shut up," yelled his wife.

I said, "How will you show your face to your people? Will this not affect your son's career? What is your earning? How can you fulfill their dreams?"

"She is right. We have to accept her proposal," said Trishna's mother firmly.

Her husband was silent. But her daughter Trishna held her mother's hand in disagreement.

"No mom. Please," Trishna requested her mother.

"You shut up too," said her mother. "What did you do with your freedom? We sent you here to pursue your dreams and you… you walked hand in hand with guys. You ditched us actually. It is all your sin. Look Trishna, one crore is a huge amount. Think about your younger brother," she said hysterically.

Trishna turned her face away in sorrow.

"Don't you worry, ma'am. We will withdraw our charges tomorrow. It is no use crying over spilt milk," said Trishna's mother.

Everybody was silent.

"Thank you very much, sister," I said with tears in my eyes.

Trishna gave me a heart-wrenching look.

Coral and his friends were soon released. They were very happy.

We hurriedly moved towards the exit door. Suddenly, the circle officer interrupted us. "I know the truth, madam. Your son is not innocent. Beware, you are feeding an animal," he said, in a very intense voice.

"Everything looks yellow to a jaundiced eye but the innocent people have nothing to fear. Anyway, thanks for your concern. I will take care of my son and you take care of this city," I replied in irritation.

He smiled and we moved away.

On the way home, we visited the Hanuman *mandir* to take the Almighty's blessings. At home, all our well-wishers had gathered.

Sheetal said to Coral, "You are very lucky Coral to have such a mother. She worked day and night to set you free. She is awesome."

Coral hugged me.

"I love you, dear Mimosa," he said.

"I love you too, my son. Now go and relax," I said.

Coral walked to his room. Sheetal followed him.

Mrs Gupta said, "I don't understand why these young girls nowadays shout so much about rape, when it is so adventurous and exciting. You know, it is my wildest fantasy."

And she burst into laughter.

We all laughed.

Mrs Kapoor's daughter said, "And aunty, why don't we get raped? Because we are sensible. These small town girls came here to make their future bright but they indulge in other activities. They forget their dreams and start hanging around malls and pubs; they behave indecently with guys and think they are cool. As you sow, so you reap."

Everybody agreed with her.

After some refreshments and more arguments over rape, everyone dispersed. "All's well that ends well," I thought. But I was wrong. As they say, crows do not turn white on washing.

Coral and I got busy with our lives soon. Coral started dating Sheetal. I began to shower more love on him than before.

Two months later arrived the horrible dark night.

It was December 3, 2009. It was Coral's twentieth birthday. I was in my clinic, trying to wrap up work fast. I had to shop for Coral's gift.

It was 9 p.m. I went to a gift shop. Nothing interested me. Suddenly, I saw a ceramic figurine of a woman feeding milk to a baby on her lap. I thought that was nice and bought it. I drove fast and reached home soon. I was very happy.

I could hear loud music from my flat, as I rang the doorbell. Coral opened the door.

"Happy birthday to you," I sang the birthday song and handed him his present.

Coral hugged me.

I saw the living room filled with smoke. His wicked friends were there. Coral introduced me to his friends. They were all drunk.

"Oh my God, aunty! You look damn hot. We are all your diehard fans," one of them said. All of them agreed.

Though I did not like the looks of their friends, I liked their compliments. I was delighted.

Coral asked me to dance with him. I hesitated as I felt a little awkward to dance with Coral in the presence of other boys, but I did not want to spoil Coral's mood. So I danced with him. We enjoyed a few dance numbers. I felt like a queen as I was the only woman among four guys. I obviously drew their attention.

"Enough now," I said and fell on the sofa. I was gasping for breath.

"Where is Sheetal?" I asked Coral.

"She has gone to her cousin's engagement," said Coral.

One of the guys fixed drinks. They offered me a drink.

"No, no I am not in the mood," I declined.

"Please mom, one peg only," Coral insisted.

"You know I prefer vodka or wine."

"Can't you drink a single peg of Scotch on your son's birthday?"

"Okay, my son. Anything for you."

We raised our glasses for a toast.

I took a sip and said, "Okay guys, I am going to sleep now. You enjoy."

"Okay mom."

I went to my room and placed the glass on a side table. I undressed and took a shower. I then wore my night gown. I finished my drink and started reading a magazine. As I was tired, I soon drifted into a deep sleep.

Suddenly, I felt a gluttonous sensation in my body. I dreamt of Dhruva.

His action made me covetous. With an earnest desire, I tried to stretch my limbs. But I was unable to move my body.

My conscience alerted me. It was not a dream. In acute fear, I opened my eyes.

Someone was over me and sucking my lips. I instantly shook my head.

It was Coral. His friends had tied my hands.

"What are you doing. You idiot!" I yelled.

He firmly pressed his hand on my mouth.

"Please mom, don't shout. Don't you know how much I love you, how much I want you? Your hot body always excites me. You are my wildest fantasy, mom. Let me fuck you and you enjoy yourself. Otherwise, I will do it forcefully and you will regret it."

I was crying. I screamed and appealed to Coral. "Please my dearest son, this is not right. This is madness. My son can't be so shameless. You are a gentle and a very decent boy. You are my blood. You are very drunk; that's why you are behaving insanely. I am begging you, please don't do this to me."

I was suffering beyond words.

"I can't control my excitement right now. You are very juicy and stimulating. Only a fool can kick away such a beauty and I am not a fool," he said like a rake.

I gathered all my strength and pushed him with my legs. But they were four. One guy quickly tied my legs. He was strong. I could not move my hands and my legs. They spread my legs.

Coral undressed me with greedy eyes. Oh my God, I shuddered in shock. My own son was invading my dignity. He was violating his source of birth.

I yelled with intense grief, "I am your mother, Coral."

"We are mother fuckers," they shouted together.

I soon surrendered. There was no use crying in wilderness. They attacked my body like carnivorous animals. They played with my body as though I was some kind of live toy. But I was indeed lifeless. They penetrated every hole in my body. My front, my back, my mouth and even my nostrils. It was the heights of insanity. I was senseless. Or were they senseless?

After besmearing my femininity and maternity with their dirty fluid, they went away contented.

I lay on bed, naked and all alone, with a badly kneaded body, trampled dignity and a crumbling soul.

I was sobbing in grief as I gazed at the ceiling with bewildered eyes.

Am I a woman? Am I a mother? Am I a whore? Who am I?

I screamed inside. My heart was roaring in grief. Tears fell from eyes. I was hissing like a wounded animal. I couldn't believe that this is what my own son had thought of me the whole time. I had been feeding an animal.

Why did I not understand Trishna's heart-wrenching look? Why did I not understand her affliction, pain, grief and anger? How could I have been so insensitive?

I lamented, "He jests at scars who never felt a wound." I burst out with great regret. Crying helped me calm down. But I was burning inside in anger, vengeance and hatred. Somehow I gathered myself and walked slowly towards the washroom.

I had no control over my tears. They were falling continuously. I placed my body inside the bathtub. I drowned up to my neck in cold water, in the biting cold weather. I was shivering.

I gritted my teeth in rage. Millions of sharp needles pierced my body. I locked my jaw tight. I had to be strong, I told myself.

I had to teach my son a lesson. A lesson he would never forget. I had to teach those bastards how to treat a woman and not see them as objects. I had to do something that would make rapists horripilate in fear. But how could I achieve this? After all, Coral was my beloved son.

I firmly decided that I had put an end to the relationship with Coral. I had to stop the motherly affection from surfacing again. I had to destroy the love I had for him. I had to kill the maternal feelings I had for him.

I came out of the tub and wiped my body calmly. I saw the time. It was 6.30 a.m.

I walked towards Coral's room. I was naked. But without any hesitation, I reposed myself very close to Coral. He was sleeping.

I kissed him unwillingly. He opened his eyes, excited and amazed.

"You were right. We must enjoy. Now you will see my fire, sweetheart," I said.

He stretched his limbs in zeal. I unbuttoned him. I sat on his masculinity.

Now, I fucked him. He enjoyed it shamelessly. I shuddered at the painful realization that I had nurtured this demon. I had helped an ungrateful creature. How stupid I had been!

Tears fell from my eyes. Tears of lost pride, fallen grace and dignity.

He did not even last a minute. His masculinity vomited.

"This was awesome," he said.

I smiled sardonically.

"Will you please pick me up from my clinic today?" I asked.

"When?"

"At 8.30 pm."

"As you wish, sweetheart," he said and hugged me.

That evening, Coral reached my clinic on time. I was listening to music on my headphone. He had come along with one of his wicked friends.

"Let's move dear," he said.

"What is the hurry?" I asked.

"Nothing, we just wanted to watch a movie with you."

"Sit. I will show you a live blue film here," I said.

"Really?" He was amazed.

Coral and his friend sat on the chairs. They were excited.

"Where are the other two?" I asked casually.

"Oh, they are busy today with their girlfriends," Coral's friend said.

I offered them a drink.

I made two large glasses of Scotch and stirred them.

The two boys insisted I make a drink for myself too.

I showed them a bottle of vodka.

"I drink vodka," I said.

They smiled.

I made a drink for myself.

We cheered.

I smiled as I enjoyed my drink.

They went into deep sleep.

I waited eagerly outside the cabin.

Two bodies were resting on two beds inside the cabin. Suddenly, I saw some movement in a body.

I smiled. It was Coral. He was naked.

He looked around in amazement. He touched his body in excitement. He then began to shiver in fear. He slowly walked towards the mirror in the room.

I could see him though he didn't see me. For he could see only himself. As he saw his body in the mirror, his eyes extended in horror.

There were female genitals in a male's body. A man's soul was trapped in a woman's genitalia. I had transformed him.

He looked ugly. Tears of lost grace fell from his eyes.

His friend's body did not show any movement. Maybe he had died, due to overdose of female hormones.

I laughed and said, "Can you rape Trishna now?"

I left the place forever.

Chapter - 3

UNBURDENED

She wiped my tears.

"I cannot see your tears, Kunwar," she said.

"They are flowing without my knowledge. I did not cry," I said, a little embarrassed.

She laughed.

"Look who is crying. It is the blinking idiot. It's you who made me content and vigorous, destroyed all my burdens and decorated me with my lost grace. I feel so comfortable with you. That's why I could share my horribly odious past with you very easily. I don't care about my past now. I am happy," she said.

"You are a woman of this millennium. I salute you. Your story fills me with compassion," I said.

"You know, today is Coral's birthday. The third of December. Last year, around the same time, it was a horrible night for me, but this time it has been amazing. I will never forget my day of awakening," she said in joy.

"You know, today is my birthday too," I said.

"Oh my God! Really?" she yelled in pleasure.

She painted my lips with her colorful lips.

"Why did not you tell me before?" she asked me.

"Does it matter? Look, I live my everyday like it is my birthday," I said, intoxicated by her juicy lips.

"Very funny, Kunwar *ji*."

She pinched my nose with affection.

"How come you came here? I mean it's not an appropriate place for you," I asked.

"I reached Kolkata with a tired soul to live with my parents. Then I wondered what I was doing. How could I explain to my parents what had happened to me? So I went to a friend, who runs an NGO for women's welfare. I joined her. One day, our team visited this place for an awareness program on AIDS. I met Meenakshi. We both liked each other. One thing that always hunted my mind was why do people commit rape? This thought became an obsession in my mind. What provokes people to do such an abominable act? I found this a good place to understand men's sexual behavior, their intimate and dark feelings and what they really think about a woman. I have to jump into the filth to pick a lotus, right?"

I interrupted her.

"That's how I picked you."

She laughed aloud in delight.

"Oh my God Kunwar, you can win anyone's heart."

"Really? Did I win your heart?" I teased her.

"Can't you see? My heart is dancing to your tune. Mr Blinking Idiot," she said sonorously.

We both laughed.

"Did you sleep with anyone other than me? I mean, at this place?"

"No. Actually, my coming here is a secret. I have not even informed my friend. Only Meenakshi knows my agenda. When I came to this place, I offered her money and free treatment to the girls. She agreed to the treatment, but she did not accept my money. She also wanted me to train the girls in refined manners and how to protect themselves from people who try to take advantage of them. She told me I could stay here for free and also sleep with men of my choice, if I wanted to. I have met many men here, but I did not dare to sleep with any of them. Maybe it is my conscience that has been controlling me. Gradually, the people here became my new family. And this place became my new address. And then, you came along. You attracted me. You charmed me. You shook my suppressed feelings violently with your childlike acts. You inflamed my lust. Do you know what I thought when I first saw you?"

"How would I know? You tell me."

"You won't believe this," she said and laughed.

"Please don't confuse me. Speak clearly. I believe you," I said eagerly.

"When I came into this room with the girls, I first looked at Meenakshi. She secretly signaled to me that you were divine and that you were the best."

"Oh my God! How do you girls talk in sign language?" I asked in disbelief.

"Anyway, I thought I should check you out and see if you were an impostor or you really got something. I was judging you but you dazzled me. When I came back to my senses, I was a changed person."

"Do you know what I felt when I first saw you?"

"What?" This time she was eager.

"I thought I was falling into a pit full of dung. As I fell into it, I found my lost mobile phone in there."

"Oh my God! You are so rude. You compared me to a mobile phone. I won't talk to you."

I laughed aloud.

"Well, the mobile is the most precious thing today."

"I don't believe you," she pretended to be angry.

"Look, nowadays mobile phones come with a tracker. Have you heard of diamonds with trackers? So which one is more precious? Anyway, I was just kidding."

We laughed.

"No one can win against you," she said.

"But you have won me, Mimosa," I said with compassion.

She embraced me with intense affection.

We slept peacefully that night. In the morning, we heard the door unlock.

Meenakshi and Pandey entered the room. Thankfully, we had dressed up already.

"Oh my dear, you are looking so very beautiful," Meenakshi said to Mimosa.

"Was I wrong?" she asked Mimosa.

Mimosa smiled in modesty. They both laughed.

"So Pandey. Did you enjoy?" I asked Pandey.

"Oh yes sir," he said, in hesitation.

"He is useless, Krishna. His weapon does not fire," Meenakshi interrupted.

We all laughed aloud. Pandey was embarrassed.

I counted forty five-hundred rupee notes and handed them to Pandey.

"Don't take it, Meenakshi," Mimosa said.

"Did I ask for payment?" Meenakshi asked Pandey.

"Yesterday was his birthday," Mimosa announced, pointing towards me.

"Oh my God," said Meenakshi and caressed me affectionately.

Pandey was confused.

"This is not right. This is your job, Meenakshi *ji*," I requested.

"It's not about a job, it's about the heart. Talk to Mona. I don't know anything," said Meenakshi.

"Please," I said to Mimosa.

"Look Kunwar. I have always been grateful to useless people in my life. For the first time, I am really grateful to a truly deserving person. It's priceless what you gave me. I don't want to ruin my happiness for these pieces of paper pieces," she said intensely.

Tears filled my eyes. I hugged her.

"Okay, I have an idea," I said.

"What?"

"It is my birthday. So let us all celebrate today with this money. It is my treat. Let us have a pizza party. Hurray!" I yelled.

"You are impossible," Mimosa said and laughed mildly.

"And Meenakshi, my sir is very fond of *mujra*. That is why he came here, but I don't understand why he chose her. He is not like us," said Pandey.

Meenakshi was very happy.

"Oh, it's simple. Let us all celebrate Krishna's birthday. Today will be great fun," Meenakshi said enthusiastically.

"So accept this money," I said and saw the clock. It was 8.30 a.m.

"Shops will not be open now," I said.

Meenakshi laughed.

"You know, everybody, from a *rickshawala* to a wealthy businessman, visits this place. So don't worry, one phone call is sufficient to make all the arrangements," she said with pride.

"That's great," I said. "Pandey, please do me a favor."

"Yes sir, tell me."

"Please go to my hotel and bring my luggage here. And ask for my return flight ticket at the reception. I have paid for everything."

"Okay sir," said Pandey and left.

"May I sleep now? I am exhausted," I said to Mimosa.

"Oh yes. Why not? Get some sound sleep. We are going," said Meenakshi.

Turning to Mimosa, she said, "Let's go, Mimosa. We have to decorate this place. Lots of work."

"Please wake me up when Pandey comes back," I said to Mimosa.

"Sure," she said and left the room with Meenakshi.

I knew she was leaving the room against her will.

I opened my eyes to a soft affectionate touch that tickled my heart. It was Mimosa. Her fingers were caressing my hair. Our eyes met and time stood still. When I came to my senses, her lips were imprinted on mine. I stretched my limbs as I drowned in the intoxication of an imperishable drink.

I smiled and so did she.

"You are a cutie," she said in delight.

"What time is it?" I asked, still drowsy.

"It's 11 a.m. now, Mr Cutie Pie. You know, I have been sitting here for two hours. It was fun to watch you sleep. You make too many faces during sleep, like a child," she said and laughed.

"Everyone does that," I said, a little irritated. "And why are you here? Shouldn't you be with them, helping them?"

"I was there, sweetie, but my heart was here. Meenakshi sensed it and sent me back here to take care of you. She is very smart. And, I don't know, it's very hard to stay away from you."

"But you know that I have to go today."

"I know. That's why I don't want to spend even a single moment without you."

"You won't stop me from leaving?"

"Does it matter? I know you won't stay back. I know everything now."

Meenakshi and Pandey entered the room.

"Sir, your flight is at 3.30 p.m.," Pandey said.

Meenakshi said anxiously, "You both are too lazy. Hurry Kunwar, freshen up first. And you too Mimosa, go get ready. We have only two hours. We have to give him a good time so that he remembers us for years. All the girls are ready and eager."

Mimosa looked at me with teary eyes. Her look pierced my heart.

When I entered the place of celebration, I was stunned. I felt like royalty.

Girls showered rose petals on me and sang the birthday song with energy.

In the center stood Mimosa in a gold and scarlet *lehenga*. In her hand was a silver plate with a birthday cake on it. She looked like a goddess.

I walked towards her with an open mouth. I drowned in her beauty, as I kept blinking my eyes.

"Shame on you! I am ten years older than you, Mr Blinking Idiot," she teased me.

Everyone burst into laughter. I kissed her passionately. Then I felt a bit embarrassed. They laughed again.

Then the girls performed the traditional *mujra* for me. It was like a scene from an old Bollywood movie.

I enjoyed the dance a lot. Then there was a final performance. Oh I was amazed. I was delighted. It was

Mimosa doing the *naagin* dance, her beautiful body slithering like a serpent. She was on fire. She was fabulous with her stunning looks, attitude and delicate moves. She danced for me alone. She kept smiling during the performance.

As her performance reached the end, everyone, including Meenakshi, joined her.

They were all dancing for me. I stood up and matched steps with them. As the dance ended, Mimosa gave me a beautiful gold chain and said, "It is from all of us. We have already given you our hearts. The chain is just to say you 'thank you.' Thank you for coming here. Please remember us."

Her eyes were wet. She grabbed my glass of Scotch and took a sip and passed it on to Meenakshi who passed it around to all the girls. "We are immortals now," Mimosa announced in delight.

I was stunned at their love. My actions seemed insignificant in front of the women's greatness. I felt very small in front of them. I could not control myself and I burst into tears. Tears of grace and gratitude fell from my eyes.

Grace of my virtue, grace of my pride. The women encircled me. I was overwhelmed.

Soon Pandey and I were on the road, on our way to the airport.

I was drowned in her thoughts.

"How did she know that I love the *naagin* tune?" I asked Pandey.

He laughed.

"Sir, actually they asked me what you like the most. As since I knew it, I told them."

"Oh you don't know Pandey what I have left behind."

"Just forget it, sir."

I ignored him as I picked up a newspaper from the dashboard.

"Is it today's?" I asked him.

"Yes sir. I bought it when I went to the hotel to pick up your luggage."

"Okay."

I read the headline. "Five men gangrape a seven-year-old girl in UP"

"Mother fuckers," I whispered.

"What happened sir?"

"These rapists, Pandey. These bastards are mentally ill."

"What sir? These girls provoke them actually. They wear such dresses that men cannot control themselves."

"You idiot! How can you explain rape on minors?"

He answered shamelessly. "You are also a man, sir. That's why those whores were hovering around you. You know once our *baba* (penis) becomes a rocket, it starts searching for a vacant space to fire into."

"Oh my God, I thought, "I have to talk to him in his language."

"Okay Pandey, let us answer this. Assume four drunken stouts hire your car."

"Okay sir," Pandey said smiling.

"They are excessively drunk."

"Okay sir." He was still smiling.

"They do not see a single girl."

"Okay sir."

"Their *baba* becomes a rocket suddenly."

"Okay sir."

"In their insanity, they grab you and start firing their rockets, one by one in your bloody asshole. It is not enough. So they push an iron rod inside your hole as they want to discover something in your ass. How would you feel? Don't forget, you too have a hole," I yelled at him in anger.

His smile vanished as he imagined the scene I just described to him. I could see him shivering in fear. There was pin drop silence.

"How can you be so insensitive, Pandey? You know you give her one, she returns to you ten. Fun must happen with consent, not by force."

"Sorry sir, I was wrong."

"Rape is a mental sickness actually."

"How can it be cured, sir?"

"There are very few incidents of planned rape. Normally, it happens due to a sudden burst of sexual desire. So it can't be cured but it can be prevented."

"How sir?"

"Look outside. Look at the green boards on the roads."

He looked and read them aloud.

"Go slow, a family is waiting. Don't drink and drive."

"Do you follow these rules?" I asked.

"Yes sir. The boards alert me. So I drive carefully."

"That's my point."

"What do you mean, sir?"

"DOGS AND RAPISTS NOT ALLOWED. Cover every public and isolated place with these hoardings. Put them up at schools, hospitals, hotels, parks, railway stations, everywhere. They will alert the mind and hopefully control any sudden burst of sexual desire. When the British compared us to dogs, we came to our senses and fought together for our freedom. DOGS AND INDIANS NOT ALLOWED. This sentence inflamed our pride and our collective wisdom. It was a powerful sentence."

"But what if rape happens in spite of these signboards?" Pandey asked, driving carefully.

"What is the first legal action when a person kills another person intentionally with his car, other than arresting him? What will happen to his licensed weapon?" I asked him.

"The driver's license is cancelled," answered Pandey mechanically. Suddenly, his eyes were wide open as he understood my point.

"Oh my God! You want to make rapists impotent?" he asked, a bit startled.

"No, I want their transformation," I said, vociferously.

"What do you mean, sir?"

"Look, it is not a man's organs that invade a woman's genitals. It is his intention that rapes her soul. His masculinity violates her femininity. When a man has a violent and wrong desire for a woman's body, give him that. Convert him into her. Transform those bastards," I said, grinding my teeth.

Pandey kept quiet. He was horrified.

Soon we reached the airport. Pandey brought the car to a halt. I got out of the car and thanked him for everything. Pandey smiled.

As I started walking towards the entry, Pandey yelled suddenly, "I will write it on my cars."

"What?" I screamed.

"DOGS AND RAPISTS NOT ALLOWED," he yelled again.

I smiled.